ALTERNATOR BOOKS™

SERENA WILLIAMS

TENNIS SUPERSTAR

NIKI AHRENS

Lerner Publications ◆ Minneapolis

For relentless learners

Lerner Publications Company
An imprint of Lerner Publishing Group, Inc.
241 First Avenue North
Minneapolis, MN 55401 USA

For reading levels and more information, look up this title at www.lernerbooks.com.

Main body text set in Aptifer Sans LT Pro.
Typeface provided by Linotype AG.

Library of Congress Cataloging-in-Publication Data

Names: Ahrens, Niki, 1979– author.
Title: Serena Williams : tennis superstar / Niki Ahrens.
Description: Minneapolis : Lerner Publications, 2022 | Series: Boss lady bios (Alternator Books) | Includes bibliographical references and index. | Audience: Ages 8–12 | Audience: Grades 4–6 | Summary: "Serena Williams is one of the world's greatest tennis players. She also designs clothing, invests in startups, and raises her daughter. Learn how the superstar does it all and still finds time to help others"— Provided by publisher.
Identifiers: LCCN 2020052727 (print) | LCCN 2020052728 (ebook) | ISBN 9781728404547 (library binding) | ISBN 9781728417684 (ebook)
Subjects: LCSH: Williams, Serena, 1981—Juvenile literature. | African American women tennis players—Biography—Juvenile literature. | Tennis players—United States—Biography—Juvenile literature.
Classification: LCC GV994.W55 A37 2022 (print) | LCC GV994.W55 (ebook) | DDC 796.342092 [B]—dc23

LC record available at https://lccn.loc.gov/2020052727
LC ebook record available at https://lccn.loc.gov/2020052728

Manufactured in the United States of America
1-48512-49026-3/22/2021

TABLE OF CONTENTS

Serena Williams serves the ball during the 2017 Australian Open.

NUMBER ONE AGAIN

THE CROWD AT THE 2017 AUSTRALIAN OPEN CHEERED WILDLY. Serena Williams prepared her serve for the champion point. The opponent facing her across the tennis court was her sister Venus Williams. This match would determine the winner of the Open. The tournament is one of the four most important annual tennis tournaments, called the majors. The four majors together are named the Grand Slam.

On her second serve attempt, Williams sent the ball to her sister's court. The ball whizzed back and forth across the net until her sister hit it out of bounds. The audience roared and rose to their feet. Williams had won the Australian Open. The victory was her twenty-third major championship, a world record in the Open Era. Her sister hugged Williams as the crowd thundered with applause.

Williams's persistence and dedication to tennis have enabled her to accomplish feats no one else in the sport has. Over her career, she honed her serve to one of the greatest of all time. She was ranked the number one women's tennis player in the world for more than three consecutive years. Williams is a four-time Olympic gold medalist who has changed the sport forever. But she also works to change more than tennis.

Serena Williams (*right*) hugs her sister Venus Williams after defeating her in the tournament final.

Serena (*right*) and Venus in Oakland, California, in 1994

CHAPTER 1
GROWING UP ON THE COURT

SERENA JAMEKA WILLIAMS WAS BORN ON SEPTEMBER 26, 1981, IN SAGINAW, MICHIGAN. She lived with her four older sisters and parents, Richard Williams and Oracene Price. Before Serena turned two years old, her family moved to California. Her father had a detailed plan to raise his children to be tennis champions. When Serena was three years old, her

Elite athletes often start their sport at a young age and train for many hours each day.

father introduced her to tennis. During their training, he repeated, "Just look at the ball, Serena," and "just swing." Both her parents coached her.

Serena and her sisters practiced on tennis courts around the cities of Compton and Lynwood, in Southern California. When Serena was four, she competed in her first tournament. She played in local tournaments in California for the next five years.

Serena was nine years old when Rick Macci, a top tennis coach, invited her and Venus to train at his tennis academy in Florida. Taking a chance, the family moved across the country. Macci made Serena's practice sessions especially difficult. Serena had to use tennis balls with less bounce and return balls blasting toward her at 100 miles (161 km) per hour. But Macci believed that Serena's determination to win set her apart. She practiced four to five hours a day at the tennis academy after her school day ended at one in the afternoon.

Delray Beach, Florida, where Macci's tennis academy moved in 1992

In Florida, Serena practiced tennis at a resort. Resorts and country clubs often have tennis courts on their premises.

Young Serena navigated between different worlds. She attended a poorer school but played tennis at a first-rate resort. When the tennis academy moved two hours south to Delray Beach, Florida, Serena's family moved with it. The Williams family spent all of their free time on the courts, morning till night, and even ate their lunches there.

Serena's faith was also a big part of her life. She was raised as a Jehovah's Witness and has remained a member of the church. She later wrote that playing tennis and attending services at the family's Kingdom Hall were "like breathing" for her.

Fourteen-year-old Serena debuted as a professional tennis player in Quebec, Canada. But her first pro tournament didn't go well. Defeated, Serena learned that she had to work even harder to win at a high level. She dedicated herself to growing her tennis skills. It was more than a year before she competed professionally again.

Kingdom Halls are where Jehovah's Witnesses worship. Serena's faith has always been important to her.

YOU'RE THE BOSS

You can always improve a skill. Think about some of the things you do well, or would like to learn. Maybe you know how to play a sport or musical instrument. What would you like to become better at?

To increase your skill, dedicate time and effort to practicing that activity. During each practice session, focus on one specific thing, such as keeping a musical beat or your balance while doing a karate form. Challenge yourself to get better at that technique. Some things will feel hard at first. But keep trying and believe you can do it. Have fun watching your progress! Soon you'll accomplish something new.

Williams at the US Open in 1999

CHAPTER 2
RISING STAR

SERENA RETURNED TO PRO TENNIS AT THE AGE OF FIFTEEN. She had ups and downs. In her second professional match, she lost in the first round of singles. But at the same tournament, she went all the way to the quarterfinals in doubles with Venus. This success gave Serena more confidence in her abilities.

The following year, she played her first major match at the 1998 Australian Open. After winning her first match, she faced none other than her sister Venus. Serena lost, but competing at a high level against Venus was an inspiring experience for her. Serena looked up to her older sister and wanted to follow in her footsteps to play great tennis. Serena ended 1998 ranked among the world's top 20 tennis players.

Serena serves to Venus at the Australian Open in 1998. Competing against her sister inspired her.

Tennis star Althea Gibson holding her national tennis championship trophies in 1957. Gibson was another inspiration for Williams.

In 1999 she won the US Open, her first major championship. She was the second Black woman to win the tournament, after Althea Gibson won in 1957 and 1958. Williams went on to represent the United States in the 2000 Summer Olympic Games, where she and her sister teamed up to win the gold medal in doubles.

By the end of the year, Williams ranked fourth among tennis players worldwide. Venus Williams ranked third. The sisters became each other's toughest competitors.

Not all the attention Williams received was positive. In 2001 she returned to the Indian Wells, California, tournament, where she had relaunched her pro career four years earlier. She heard angry booing and racist name-calling. Some shouted for her to return to Compton.

Venus Williams (*right*) beat Williams (*left*) to win the 2001 US Open

The hostility and racism directed at her hurt her and her concentration. She finished the tournament. But for herself and for little girls watching, Williams took a stand and refused to return to Indian Wells for over fifteen years.

The Williams sisters were unique in their tennis success and gained a huge audience together.

The Williams sisters faced each other in the 2001 US Open. They were the first sisters since 1884 to meet as the two finalists. They had captured the public eye: 22.7 million people watched Williams lose to her older sister.

"I REALLY THINK A CHAMPION IS DEFINED NOT BY THEIR WINS, BUT BY HOW THEY CAN RECOVER WHEN THEY FALL."

GETTING IT DONE!

In 2002 Williams ranked number one in the world in women's tennis. She won four majors in a row and was the reigning champion in each for a year. Her remarkable accomplishment was named the Serena Slam.

Williams models a dress from her first clothing line, Aneres, in 2003.

CHAPTER 3

OFF AND ON THE COURT

OFF THE COURT, WILLIAMS PURSUED HER LIFELONG INTEREST IN FASHION. She attended design and fashion classes at the Art Institute in Fort Lauderdale, Florida. She soon developed and launched her own clothing line called Aneres, her name spelled backward.

While filming a television show in 2003, Williams heard tragic news. Her oldest sister, Yetunde Price, was shot to death while riding in a car in Compton. Williams's grief over the loss, combined with her recovery from a knee injury, kept her from wanting to play tennis for a long time.

Williams (*right*) and her sister Yetunde Price

Williams reaches to return the ball at the 2005 Australian Open.

She felt conflicted during her return to tennis. She won and lost matches. Her 2005 season was going well, and she won her second Australian Open. But on the inside, Williams was struggling. She sought treatment for depression and continued to need treatment for her knee injury. She went from being ranked number 1 down to 139.

In 2006 Williams took a trip to Africa, seeking to understand her roots. She traveled to Ghana and Senegal with her mom and two of her sisters, Isha and Lyn Price. The family worked to set up tennis clinics in villages. With Senegal's president, Williams planned to help build a school that young children could attend for free. She felt she could make meaningful change one

Williams teaches tennis at a camp in Dakar, Senegal, in 2006.

Williams celebrates her quarterfinal win at the 2007 Australian Open.

child and one school at a time. She left Africa feeling stronger both off and on the tennis court. She later said of the trip, "Africa lifted me . . . and set me back down a positive path."

Feeling recharged, she won her third Australian Open in 2007. The following year, the Williams sisters won another Olympic gold medal in doubles. She also returned to Africa. But soon she faced more challenging health crises. In 2010 she underwent surgery for a cut on her foot. Then, in 2011, she needed emergency surgery for a life-threatening blood clot in her lungs. Her recoveries required an eleven-month absence from tennis.

Returning to tennis in 2012, Williams changed up her game. She trained with coach Patrick Mouratoglou that summer and beyond. Her hard work paid off with ten more major championships, including a second Serena Slam in the 2014–2015 season.

GETTING IT DONE!

In the summer of 2012, Williams won the Olympic singles gold medal and her third Olympic doubles gold medal.

Williams playing at the US Open in 2020

CHAPTER 4

GAME CHANGER

WILLIAMS WAS NAMED *SPORTS ILLUSTRATED* SPORTSPERSON OF THE YEAR IN 2016. By 2017 the thirty-five-year-old had won twenty-three major tournaments, the only player to do so since the Open Era began in 1968. Winning the Australian Open that year made her the oldest player to win a major title.

In September 2017, Williams gave birth to a daughter, Alexis Olympia Ohanian Jr. After recovering from near-death complications following the birth, Williams married Olympia's father, Alexis Ohanian, in November. She returned to world tennis and reached the finals in four more majors.

Her ambitions on and off the court remain strong, and her achievements extend beyond tennis. In 2018 she launched another clothing line called S by Serena. She has more than twenty-nine million social media

Williams's husband, Alexis Ohanian, and their daughter, Olympia

followers across platforms. In addition to helping underserved children to attend school, she's used her status to take stances against racial, gender, and socioeconomic injustices in the United States.

Many fans have called Williams the greatest tennis player of all time. Her passion and commitment to tennis, and her dedication to making it more inclusive, have changed the sport forever. She continues to play

Williams focuses intently on the court in August 2020.

at the highest level. Meanwhile, her daughter, Olympia, followed her mom's path by beginning tennis lessons at the age of three.

Williams is optimistic about what's next for her. "Maybe tennis is just a way for me to get from where I was to where I'm going," she said.

"THE DAY I STOP FIGHTING FOR EQUALITY AND FOR PEOPLE THAT LOOK LIKE YOU AND ME WILL BE THE DAY I'M IN MY GRAVE."

GETTING IT DONE!

Williams won her twenty-third major in 2017 while she was pregnant.

TIMELINE

1981 Serena Williams is born in Saginaw, Michigan, on September 26.

1995 She makes her debut as a professional tennis player.

1999 She wins the Australian Open, her first major win.

2002 She ranks number one in the world for the first time.

2002–2003 She achieves her first Grand Slam, called the Serena Slam.

2003 She releases her first clothing line, Aneres.

2017 She becomes a mother to Alexis Olympia Ohanian Jr. and marries Alexis Ohanian.

2018 She launches S by Serena, her second clothing line.

2019 She finishes as the runner-up at two major tournaments.

GLOSSARY

debut: to make a first or formal entrance

doubles: a tennis match with two-person teams opposing each other

feat: an act of skill that requires lasting effort

Grand Slam: the world's top four annual tennis championships—the Australian Open, French Open, Wimbledon, and the US Open

inclusive: including everyone, especially those excluded historically

match: a series of tennis rounds in a game of tennis that a player or team wins

Open Era: the current era of pro tennis. It began in 1968 when the majors allowed pro and amateur players to compete against one another.

opponent: a competitor facing someone in a match

singles: a tennis match with one player opposing another player

underserved: provided with inadequate service

SOURCE NOTES

7 Merlisa Lawrence Corbett, *Serena Williams: Tennis Champion, Sports Legend, and Cultural Heroine* (Lanham, MD: Rowman & Littlefield, 2020), 10.

10 Serena Williams, *My Life: Queen of the Court*, with Daniel Paisner (London: Simon & Schuster, 2010), 9.

17 Ahmed Rizvi, "The Fall and Rise of Maturing Serena Williams," *National*, September 10, 2012, https://www.thenationalnews.com/sport/the-fall-and-rise-of-maturing-serena-williams-1.632294.

22 Corbett, *Serena Williams*, 89.

27 Corbett, 137.

27 Williams, *Queen*, 257.

LEARN MORE

Britannica Kids: Serena Williams
https://kids.britannica.com/students/article/Serena-Williams/354342

Cline-Ransome, Lesa. *Game Changers: The Story of Venus and Serena Williams*. New York: Simon & Schuster Books for Young Readers, 2018.

Fishman, Jon M. *Tennis's G.O.A.T.: Serena Williams, Roger Federer, and More*. Minneapolis: Lerner Publications, 2022.

Smith, Elliott. *Serena Williams*. Minneapolis: Lerner Publications, 2021.

Sports Illustrated Kids: Serena Williams
https://www.sikids.com/tag/serena-williams

US Open: Serena Williams
https://www.usopen.org/en_US/players/overview/wta230234.html

Wetzel, Dan. *Serena Williams*. New York: Henry Holt, 2019.

WTA Tour: Serena Williams
https://www.wtatennis.com/players/230234/serena-williams

INDEX

PHOTO ACKNOWLEDGMENTS

Image credits: AP Photo/ason Heidrich/Icon Sportswire, p. 4; AP Photo/Masahiro Sugimoto, p. 5; AP Photo/NewsBase, p. 6; microgen/iStockphoto/Getty Images, p. 7; felixmizioznikov/iStock/Getty Images, p. 8; Pgiam/Getty Images, p. 9; Jack Sullivan/Alamy Stock Photo, p. 10; AP Photo/Al Messerschmidt Archive, p. 12; AP Photo/STEVE HOLLAND, p. 13; AP Photo, p. 14; AP Photo/Mark Lennihan, p. 15; AP Photo/AMY SANCETTA, p. 16; Jeff Gross/Getty Images, p. 18; Chris Polk/FilmMagic/Getty Images, p. 19; AP Photo/RICK STEVENS, p. 20; SEYLLOU/AFP/Getty Images, p. 21; AP Photo/ROB GRIFFITH, p. 22; AP Photo/Seth Wenig, p. 24; AP Photo/Trevor Collens, p. 25; AP Photo/Timothy D. Easley, p. 26.

Front cover: AP Photo/Frank Franklin II.